ABDO Publishing Company is the exclusive school and library distributor of Rabbit Ears Books.

Library bound edition 2005.

Library of Congress Cataloging-in-Publication Data

Metaxas, Eric.
   The fisherman and his wife / written by the Brothers Grimm / adapted by Eric Metaxas ;
illustrated by Diana Bryan.
        p. cm.
   "Rabbit Ears books."
   Summary: The fisherman's greedy wife is never satisfied with the wishes granted her by
an enchanted fish.
   ISBN 1-59197-747-9
   [1. Fairy tales. 2. Folklore—Germany.] I. Grimm, Jacob, 1785-1863. II. Grimm,
Wilhelm, 1786-1859. III. Bryan, Diana, ill. IV. Fisherman and his wife. English. V. Title.

PZ8.M55Fi 2004
398.2'0943'02—dc22

                                                                              2004047326

All Rabbit Ears books are reinforced library binding
and manufactured in the United States of America.

written by The Brothers Grimm
adapted by Eric Metaxas

THE FISHERMAN AND HIS WIFE

illustrated by Diana Bryan

Rabbit Ears Books

Once upon a time there was a fisherman and his wife who lived together in a hovel by the sea. And every day the fisherman went down to the sea and fished. And he fished and he fished.

And one time he was sitting there like that with his line, staring into the glimmering water. And he sat and sat.

Then his line went to the bottom, deep underneath, and when he hauled it up, he pulled out a big flounder. Then the flounder said to him: "Hear me, fisherman. I beg you, let me live. I'm no real flounder. I'm an enchanted prince. What would you gain by killing me? I wouldn't taste right to you anyway. Put me back in the water and let me swim free."

"Well," said the fisherman, "you don't need to go on about it. I'd certainly let any flounder that could talk swim free anyway." With that he put him back into the water and the flounder went to the bottom, leaving in his wake a long streak of blood. Then the fisherman arose and returned to his wife in the hovel.

"Husband," said the wife, "didn't you catch anything today?"

"No," said the husband. "I caught a flounder who said he was an enchanted prince, so I let him swim free again."

"Didn't you wish for anything?" said the wife.

"No," said the husband. "What would I wish for?"

"Ach," said the wife, "it's awful living in a hovel that smells and is so disgusting. You could at least have asked him for a little cottage. Go back again and call to him. Tell him we wish to have a little cottage."

"Ach," said the husband, "what should I go back there for?"

"Because," said the wife, "you had him for sure and you let him swim free again. He's sure to grant it. Go there quickly."

The husband still didn't want to go, but he didn't want to argue with his wife either, so he went back to the sea.

When he got there the sea was all green and yellow and it was no longer glimmering as before. And so he went and stood by it and said:

Flounder, flounder, in the sea
Come, I bid thee, come to me.
My wife, whose name is Ilsebill,
Wants what I would never will.

Then the flounder came swimming by and said: "Well, then, what does she want?"

"Ach," said the husband, "after all, I did catch you. Now my wife says I should have wished for something. She doesn't want to live in a hovel anymore. She'd like to have a cottage."

"Go," said the flounder, "she has it already."

Then the husband went and discovered a small cottage and his wife was sitting in front of the door upon a bench. Then his wife took him by the hand and said to him: "See? Certainly now this is much better. Come inside."

Then they went in and inside the cottage there was a beautiful little parlor and a bedroom with their very own bed, and a kitchen and a larder — everything of the very best — with a cupboard and with brassware and tinware of the finest quality — everything one could expect.

And in back there was also a small barnyard with chickens and ducks and a little garden with vegetables and fruit.

"See," said the wife, "isn't that nice?"

"Yes," said the husband, "and let it remain this way and we shall live very happily."

"We'll think about that," said the wife. With that they had something to eat and went to bed.

And so it went for eight or fourteen days, and then the wife said: "Listen, husband. This cottage is much too cramped and the yard and garden are too small. The flounder could just as well have given us a bigger house. I would really like to live in a great stone castle. Go to the flounder that he might give us a castle."

"Ach, wife," said the husband, "surely this cottage is good enough. Why would we want to live in a castle?"

"Why, indeed!" said the wife. "Just go. The flounder can always do it."

"No, wife," said the husband, "the flounder has only just given us the cottage. I don't want to go to him again already. The flounder might not like it."

"Just go," said the wife. "He can certainly grant it gladly."

The husband's heart grew heavy and he didn't want to go. "It's not right," he said to himself, but he went anyway. When he got to the sea the water was all violet and dark blue and gray and thick and no longer as green and yellow as before. But it was still calm. Then he went and stood by it and said:

Flounder, flounder, in the sea
Come, I bid thee, come to me.
My wife, whose name is Ilsebill,
Wants what I would never will.

"Well then, what does she want?" said the flounder.

"Ach," said the husband, "she wants to live in a big stone castle."

"Go. She's standing in front of the gate," said the flounder.

Then the husband went, thinking he was going home to their cottage, but when he arrived, he saw a magnificent stone castle standing in its place, and his wife was standing at the top of the steps, about to go in. And she took him by the hand and said, "Come in, husband."

With that he went inside with her, and inside the castle there was a large front hall with a mosaic marble floor, and all the walls shone brightly and were hung with exquisite tapestries, and in the rooms there were chairs and tables of real gold and chandeliers were hanging from the ceilings and on the tables there was food of every kind in great abundance and wine of the very best. And behind the house there was also a large yard with horse stables and cow stalls and carriages of the highest quality and there was a large and beautiful garden with the most beautiful flowers and the finest fruit trees and a park practically a half mile long in which there were stags and does and hares and everything anyone could wish for.

"Now," said the wife, "isn't that nice?"

"Yes," said the husband, "and let it always remain this way and we shall be forever satisfied."

"We'll think about that," said the wife. "Let's sleep on it."

With that they went to bed.

The next morning the wife woke up first. It was just daylight and from her bed she could see the beautiful countryside spread out before her. Her husband was only just beginning to rouse himself, so she poked him in the ribs with her elbow and said: "Husband, get up and look out the window. Couldn't we be king over all that land? Go to the flounder that we might be king."

"Ach, wife," said the husband, "what do we want to be king for? I don't want to be king."

"Well," said the wife, "if you don't want to be king, I want to be king. Go to the flounder that I might be king."

"Ach, wife," said the husband, "why do you want to be king? I can't ask that of him."

"Why not?" said the wife. "Go directly there. I must be king."

Then he went, but he was very unhappy. "It isn't right," thought the husband. "It just is not right."

When he arrived, the sea was all black-gray and came heaving up from the depths and had a foul stench. Then he went and stood by it and said:

Flounder, flounder, in the sea
Come, I bid thee, come to me.
For my wife, whose name is Ilsebill,
Wants what I would never will.

"Well then, what does she want?" said the flounder.

"Ach," said the husband. "She wants to be king."

"Go," said the flounder. "She is already."

Then the husband went, but as he approached the castle he saw that it had grown much larger and now possessed a large tower with gorgeous ornaments upon it. And sentinels were standing in front of the gate and there were many soldiers with drums and trumpets. And when he went inside the castle everything was made of pure marble with gold and there were velvet tapestries with huge golden tassels. Then the doors of the great hall were opened and there was the entire court, and his wife was sitting upon a high throne of gold and diamonds, wearing a big golden crown. The scepter in her hand was made of pure gold and jewels, and beside her, all in a row, stood her vestal virgins, each one a head shorter than the next.

Then he went and stood there and said: "Ach, wife. Are you king now?"

"Yes," said the wife, "now I'm king."

Then he just stood there and looked at her, and when he had looked at her for a time, he said: "Ach, wife. Let's leave well enough alone, now that you're king. Now let's not wish for another thing."

"No, husband," said the wife, and she became very unsettled.

"I'm getting horribly bored. I can't bear it another minute. Go to the flounder. Now I am king, but I must be emperor also!"

"Ach, wife," said the husband, "he can't make emperors. I couldn't ask that of the flounder. There's only one emperor in the empire. He simply cannot make you emperor. He cannot, cannot do it."

"What!?" said the wife. "I am king and you are only my husband. Will you go now? Go right away. If he can make a king, he can make an emperor. I want to be emperor! Go immediately!"

And so he had to go. But he was very frightened, and he thought to himself, "This isn't going to turn out very well. Emperor is too shameless. The flounder will finally become angry."

With that he came to the sea and the sea was already completely black and thick and it began to churn up from below so that it made bubbles, and such a sharp wind blew over it that it curdled. Now the husband turned gray with fear. Then he went and stood there and said:

> Flounder, flounder, in the sea
> Come, I bid thee, come to me.
> For my wife, whose name is Ilsebill,
> Wants what I would never will.

"Well then, what does she want?" said the flounder.

"Ach, flounder," he said, "my wife wants to be emperor."

"Go," said the flounder, "she is already."

Then the husband went, and when he arrived the entire castle was made of polished marble, with statues of alabaster and ornaments of gold. Soldiers marched back and forth in front of the gate and blew trumpets and beat drums and kettledrums. When he came inside, there sat his wife upon a throne that was made out of a single piece of gold and that was fully two leagues high, and she had on a great golden crown that was three yards high and set with diamonds and carbuncles. And in one hand she held the scepter, and in the other the imperial orb. And in front of her were many princes and dukes and barons, who moved about as though they were servants. Then the husband went and stood among them and said: "Wife, are you emperor now?"

"Yes," she said, "now I'm emperor."

The husband stood there and observed her closely, and after he'd looked at her for a time he said: "Ach, wife. How nice it is, now that you're emperor."

"Husband," she said, "what are you standing there for? I am now emperor, but I want to be Pope, too! Go to the flounder."

"Ach, wife," said the husband, "what won't you wish for? You can't become Pope. There's only one Pope in all of Christendom. That the flounder cannot do."

"Husband," she said, "I must become Pope this very day!"

"No, wife," said the husband, "I cannot ask that of him. It won't end up well. The flounder cannot make you Pope!"

"What pure nonsense!" said the wife. "If he can make an emperor, he can make a Pope too! Go to him! I am the emperor and you are only my husband. Now will you go!?"

Then he was afraid, and he went. But he felt very weak, and he shivered and shook, and his knees and calves trembled. And there moved such a wind over the countryside that the clouds flew across the sky and the leaves blew down from the trees and the water roared and surged as though it were boiling and the waves smashed upon the shore. There was still a tiny bit of blue in the middle of the sky, but on the edge it was red, as though portending a heavy thunderstorm. Then he went and stood there in despair, and in fear he said:

Flounder, flounder, in the sea
Come I bid thee, come to me.
For my wife, whose name is Ilsebill,
Wants what I would never will.

"Well then, what does she want?" said the flounder.

"Ach," said the husband, "she wants to be Pope."

"Go," said the flounder. "She is already."

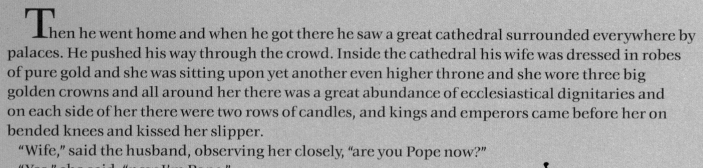

Then he went home and when he got there he saw a great cathedral surrounded everywhere by palaces. He pushed his way through the crowd. Inside the cathedral his wife was dressed in robes of pure gold and she was sitting upon yet another even higher throne and she wore three big golden crowns and all around her there was a great abundance of ecclesiastical dignitaries and on each side of her there were two rows of candles, and kings and emperors came before her on bended knees and kissed her slipper.

"Wife," said the husband, observing her closely, "are you Pope now?"

"Yes," she said, "now I'm Pope."

Then he just stood there considering her carefully, and it was as though he were gazing into the bright sun. After he had looked at her for a time, he said: "Ach, wife. How nice this is, now that you're Pope."

But she remained as perfectly stiff as an oak tree. She didn't move or stir.

Then he said, "Wife, now be satisfied. There's nothing more that you can wish for."

"I'll think about that," said the wife. With that the two of them went to bed. But she was not satisfied. She could only think of what she would become next.

The husband slept well and soundly — he'd walked quite a lot during the day — but the wife couldn't fall asleep at all. She was constantly thinking about what she could become next. But she couldn't think of a single thing. Then the sun began to rise, and when she noticed the first red light of dawn, she pulled herself up in bed and looked toward it, and when she beheld the sun rising up over the horizon, she thought, "Aha! Couldn't I also have the power to raise the sun and the moon?"

"Husband," she said, and poked him in the ribs with her elbow, "wake up and go to the flounder. I want to be like the Lord God!"

For the most part the husband was still asleep, but he became so frightened that he fell out of bed. He thought he'd misheard her and he said: "Ach, wife, what did you say?"

"Husband," she said, "if I cannot make the sun and moon rise, and see it with my own eyes that the sun and the moon rise, I won't be able to tolerate it. I won't have another hour of peace if I can't make them rise by myself."

Then she stared at him so terribly that a shudder came over him.

"Go quickly. I want to be like the Lord God!"

"Ach, wife," said the husband, falling onto his knees before her, "the flounder cannot do that. Emperor and Pope he can do, but I beg you, think it over and stay Pope."

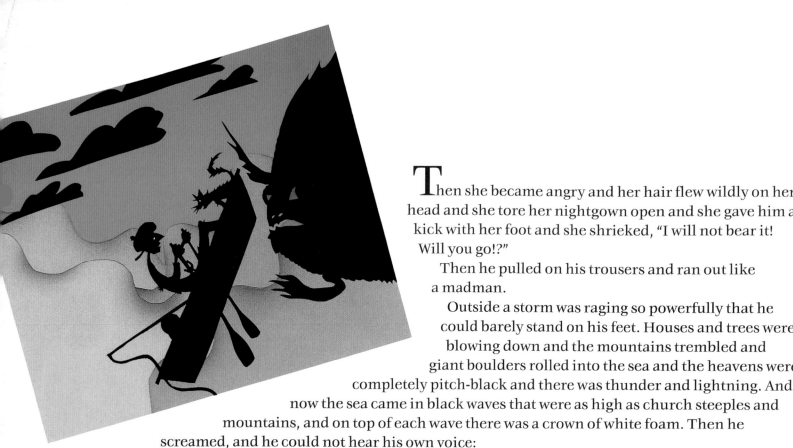

$\mathbf{T}$hen she became angry and her hair flew wildly on her head and she tore her nightgown open and she gave him a kick with her foot and she shrieked, "I will not bear it! Will you go!?"

Then he pulled on his trousers and ran out like a madman.

Outside a storm was raging so powerfully that he could barely stand on his feet. Houses and trees were blowing down and the mountains trembled and giant boulders rolled into the sea and the heavens were completely pitch-black and there was thunder and lightning. And now the sea came in black waves that were as high as church steeples and mountains, and on top of each wave there was a crown of white foam. Then he screamed, and he could not hear his own voice:

Flounder, flounder, in the sea
Come, I bid thee, come to me.
For my wife, whose name is Ilsebill,
Wants what I would never will.

"Well then, what does she want?" said the flounder.
"Ach," he said, "she wants to be like the Lord God."
"Go. She's already sitting in the hovel again."

And there they are still sitting, unto this very day.